YOU HAD ME AT DRAGONS

YOU HAD ME AT DRAGONS

Copyright © Octopus Publishing Group Limited, 2025

All rights reserved.

Text by Debbie Chapman

No part of this book may be reproduced by any means, nor transmitted, nor translated into a machine language, without the written permission of the publishers.

Condition of Sale
This book is sold subject to the condition that it shall not, by way of trade or otherwise, be lent, resold, hired out or otherwise circulated in any form of binding or cover other than that in which it is published and without a similar condition including this condition being imposed on the subsequent purchaser.

An Hachette UK Company
www.hachette.co.uk

Summersdale Publishers
Part of Octopus Publishing Group Limited
Carmelite House
50 Victoria Embankment
LONDON
EC4Y 0DZ
UK

This FSC® label means that materials and other controlled sources used for the product have been responsibly sourced

www.summersdale.com

The authorized representative in the EEA is Hachette Ireland, 8 Castlecourt Centre, Dublin 15, D15 XTP3, Ireland (email: info@hbgi.ie)

Printed and bound in Poland

ISBN: 978-1-83799-932-3
eISBN: 978-1-83799-933-0

Substantial discounts on bulk quantities of Summersdale books are available to corporations, professional associations and other organizations. For details contact general enquiries: telephone: +44 (0) 1243 771107 or email: enquiries@summersdale.com.

YOU HAD ME AT DRAGONS

Smouldering Quotes and Passionate
Affirmations for Romantasy Fans

Me: Looking for a hero

Also me: Only interested if he's a shadow daddy with a tragic backstory and a bad attitude

Get in the mood

When you're reading, your imagination is doing most of the hard work – and one of the joys of romantasy is that it can whisk you away to another world, even if you're reading on a commuter train or snatching 5 minutes on your lunch break in the office. But when you do want to settle in for full-scale immersion, to make your reading session extra-special, why not set the scene with a soft fur rug, your favourite incense, gentle mood lighting and plenty of cozy blankets to cocoon you when you swoon. You could further feel the part by draping yourself in your most romantastic outfit and putting on some dark, sultry lipstick.

I'm more than willing to let you burn me.

REBECCA YARROS, *IRON FLAME*

His name tasted of fire and wings, of curling smoke, of subtlety and strength and the rasping whisper of scales.

Naomi Novik, *Uprooted*

I will be your God, your Creator, your Destroyer, and every depraved dark thing in between.

Kerri Maniscalco,
Throne of the Fallen

WILL SELL MY SOUL FOR A MAGICAL BOND WITH A BROODING WARRIOR

The air around him almost seemed to glimmer, gold dust in the dark. Moonlight made him more beautiful, yes, but in the same way that darkness emphasized a flame.

HANNAH WHITTEN,
THE FOXGLOVE KING

If this was weakness, he wanted to be weak. If this was sin, let him be damned to hell.

KRISTEN CICCARELLI, *REBEL WITCH*

Feral dragonrider
energy only

Love and hate are oil and water, separate but similar, and sometimes they swirl together, making it difficult to tell one from the other.

SAARA EL-ARIFI, *FAEBOUND*

And I wondered if love was too weak a word for what he felt, what he'd done for me. For what I felt for him.

SARAH J. MAAS,
A COURT OF MIST AND FURY

Savour the slow burn

That delicious first lingering glance might be all it takes to make you think, "They're destined to be together", and sure, you're desperate for them to realize what's clear as crystal to you. But it wouldn't be nearly so fun if they just hopped straight into bed, would it? So make a point of enjoying the simmer and relishing the build-up. It may be agony in the moment, but the more you savour every tantalizing nearly-touching, forced-proximity scene, the bigger the pay-off. Because, let's be honest, the fact that romantasy makes you want to yell at the characters and stay up all night reading to find out how they're going to fall into each other's arms is the whole reason we love it.

Avid collector of fictional soulmates and mythical beasts

He moved his lips to my ears. "I would burn for you, Morgan. You've set me aflame…" "Then let the flames consume us," I whispered back.

Briar Boleyn,
Queen of Roses

It's not a spark. It's an eternal fire that burns from deep within my heart and reaches out to you... And every moment I am not touching you, it eats my soul inside out, tearing me apart, until merely looking at you is an anguish I would only wish upon my worst enemy.

ELIZABETH HELEN, *BONDED BY THORNS*

Dreaming of riding dragons; stuck folding laundry

Our kiss was lightning and sweet thunder, and warm rain melting away the snow. We held each other with the desperation of two people unexpectedly alive in a star winter world of sorrow and death, on the cusp of turning the page into spring.

MELISSA CARUSO, *THE UNBOUND EMPIRE*

I need you more than the air in my lungs, more than the magic in my veins. I need your light and your darkness. I need you.

GILLIAN ELIZA WEST, *RUIN*

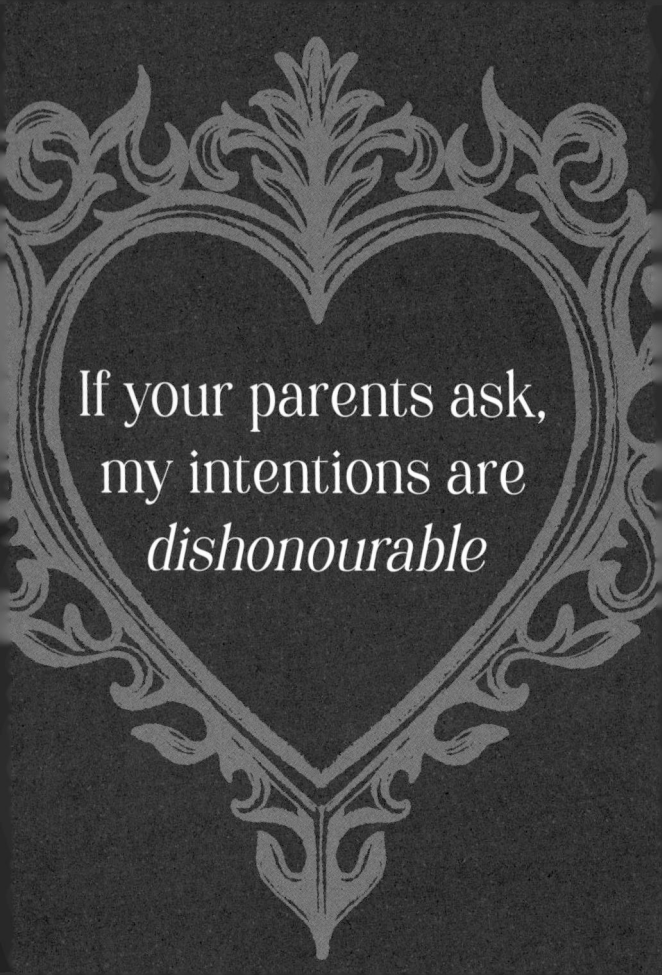

When his gaze found hers again, she could not remember how to draw breath. How beautiful, to see the exact moment he fell in love with her.

ALLISON SAFT, *WINGS OF STARLIGHT*

Highlight the good stuff

Annotating your books isn't just about making them look pretty, or showing them off on BookTok. It can also heighten your appreciation of the story and deepen your emotional connection to the characters you're reading about, as well as bring your attention to the tiny details that add up to create the whole wonderful reading experience. And, of course, it has the extra benefit of allowing you to quickly flip through all your favourite lines. Find a pen or a highlighter that won't smudge, or opt for coloured tabs, and colour-code your highlights into spicy dialogue, torturous slow-burn moments, pivotal enemies-to-lovers scenes and full-blown fae smut, so you can come back to them again and again.

> If your love only destroys, let it destroy me. I am already a doomed man.
>
> — Lyra Selene, *A Feather So Black*

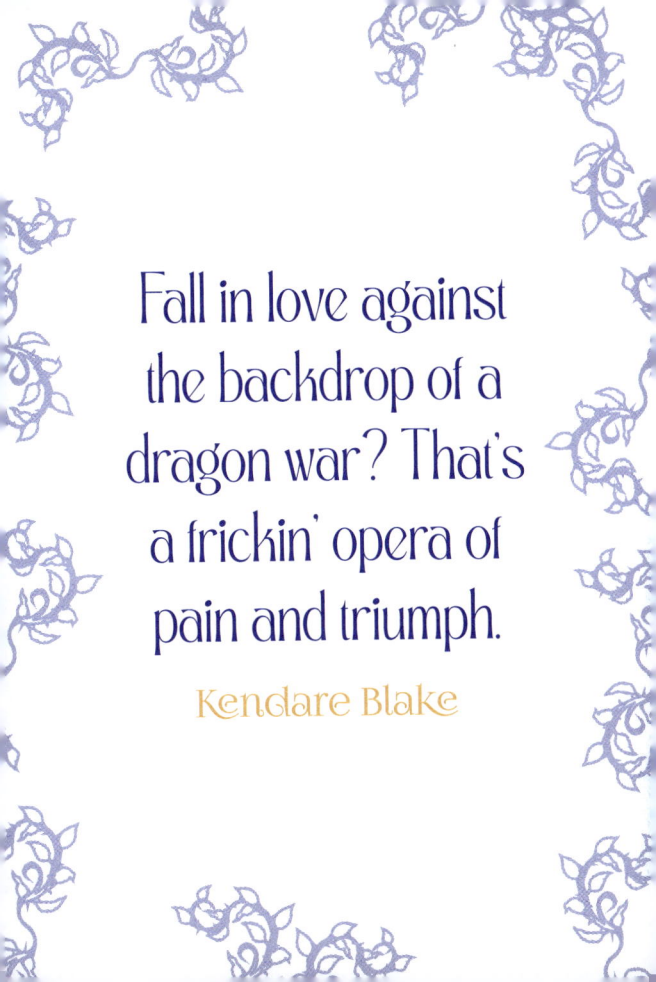

Fall in love against the backdrop of a dragon war? That's a frickin' opera of pain and triumph.

Kendare Blake

I knew he sensed it in me, too. The same desire that he'd brought to the surface of my skin the night he had touched my wings, and the night I had tasted his blood.

Carissa Broadbent, *The Ashes and the Star-Cursed King*

HERE FOR THE PLOT (AND THE SMUTTY BITS SO HOT THEY MELT MY KINDLE)

Don't you know?
Love is the purest form
of destruction there is.

AMBER V. NICOLE,
THE BOOK OF AZRAEL

It is hard to keep one's wits when faced with a woman as beautiful as the sight of shore to a man who has been lost at sea.

DANIELLE L. JENSEN, *A FATE INKED IN BLOOD*

My dream man:
tall, dark and fictional

She imagined loving him would feel like falling in love with darkness, frightening and consuming yet utterly beautiful when the stars came out.

STEPHANIE GARBER, *CARAVAL*

When his eyes meet mine, desire, as keen as any blade, bends the air between us.

HOLLY BLACK,
THE STOLEN HEIR

Romantasy trope bingo

Maybe you already keep a book journal, but have you ever tried romantasy bingo? Next time you start a new book, create a tick list of all your favourite classic romantasy tropes that you're hoping to see. Shadowy secrets? Tick. Forbidden love? Of course. A redemption arc? Bingo! Or you could make your romantasy bingo card more specific to your favourite author's tricks – maybe the lovers are always finding themselves snowed in, or the love interest just can't stop making a gruff noise deep in his throat. Lean in to the tropes!

I DUST MY SHELVES, BUT MY BOOKS ARE STILL FILTHY

She is moonlight. The mist that shrouds the mountains. The bite of electricity in the air before a storm. The smoke that rolls across a battlefield before the killing starts.

Callie Hart, *Quicksilver*

He's fire and brimstone. I'm shattered ice. Our collision is steam and destruction, destined to dissipate, but I'll gladly burn beneath him until the world comes crumbling down.

Sarah A. Parker,
When the Moon Hatched

For you, I'd steal the stars

Moon above and
earth below,
Bring my love stars
that glow.
Far past midnight,
shadows sneak;
Bring my love dreams
that speak.

SCARLETT ST. CLAIR, *KING OF BATTLE AND BLOOD*

I'll always come for you. Always. Even if the odds are against me. If you go down, I'll go down with you.

BERLYN HAYES, *PRISONERS OF BETRAYAL*

GUARD
ME LIKE A
DRAGON
PROTECTING
HIS
MOUNTAIN
OF GOLD

I was furious with the man.
So, so furious. But I also wanted to
lick his neck. It was complicated.

KATE GOLDEN, *A DAWN OF ONYX*

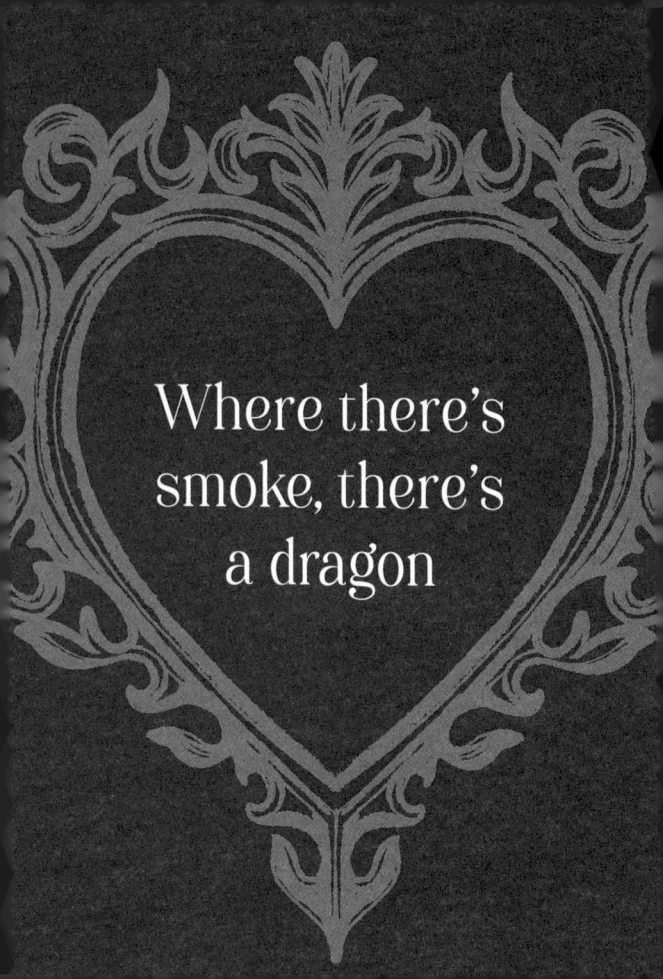

Design a fantasy world map

When you get lost in a new world, one of the most satisfying things is the cinema version of the story that plays in your head. Your imagination is running wild with ice-bound towers, ancient forests, remote fortresses, sky arenas and frozen tundras. If your current read doesn't include a map (or even if it does!), why not create your own? It can be fun to lay down on paper how you visualize the key locations in the realms of the story, or even to make up a completely new one for yourself. Look at the typical illustrations used to signify different landscapes in your favourite maps – repeating tree shapes to show enchanted woods, the architectural details of a magical academy or clifftop village – and recreate them in your very own way.

"I give you everything I have and will have," he said, entwining his fingers with hers. "I vow to love you and protect you for as long as I draw breath."

HELEN SCHEUERER, *DAWN OF MIST*

This is my last love letter to you, though some would call it a confession. I suppose both are a sort of gentle violence, putting down in ink what scorches the air when spoken aloud.

S. T. Gibson,
A Dowry of Blood

———— ✦ ———— ✦ ————

She is the embodiment of a bad decision. The twin of danger and desire. The fine line between deadly and divine. And I can feel myself drowning.

Lauren Roberts, *Powerless*

———— ✦ ———— ✦ ————

IN THE MIDDLE OF MY CHAOS, THERE YOU WERE

What girl wouldn't want to be chased by a sword wielding, angelic looking man with perfect bone structure and soul crushing eyes?

J. A. JUDE, *SUPERNOVA*

He shivers but his skin is hot, almost feverish beneath my fingers, and I think dizzily that I know exactly why Icarus flew so high: when you've spent too long in the dark, you'll melt your own wings just to feel the sun on your skin.

ALIX E. HARROW, *STARLING HOUSE*

Born from stars
and storms

She was the air I breathed, the water I drank; she was everything that made life worth living. Without her, there was nothing but darkness.

ALEXIS CALDER,
CROWN OF STARS AND FATE

> I'm no lovesick puppet, begging for a morsel of affection. I have my own dreams, my own principles, my own honour to uphold.
>
> — SUE LYNN TAN, *DAUGHTER OF THE MOON GODDESS*

Fan fiction writing contest

Challenge your friends to a fan fiction writing contest! This can either be an in-person event (give everyone a sheet of paper and a pen – or quill for added authenticity – and set the timer for 30 minutes) or digital (ask everyone to submit their 500-word short story by a certain deadline) and enjoy getting lost in each other's imaginary worlds. Fan fiction allows you to exercise your creative muscles without the hard work of dreaming up the setting and the characters. Think about the scenes you'd have liked to have seen between your favourite characters, or – depending on how smutty your friends are – imagine what happens *after* that long-lusted-for kiss.

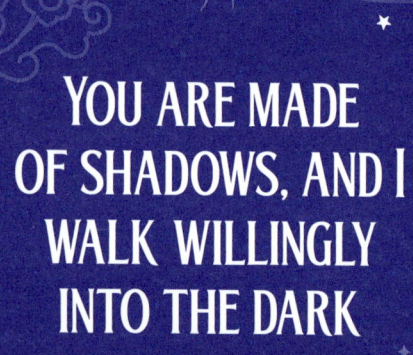

Every thought I have of you is treasonous, the way my hands ache to touch you, deceitful. Even my dreams make me a traitor of my own kingdom.

Holly Renee, *A Kingdom of Stars and Shadows*

I told you before that nothing would ever stop me from getting to you if you needed me, and that will remain true forevermore. I would tear the universe apart at its seams if I must.

Kaylie Smith, *Phantasma*

Men come and go; dragons are forever

Fire of my heart,
come that I may see you,
warm my weary bones,
be my place of rest.

CHARISSA WEAKS,
THE WITCH COLLECTOR

In this life and any other. There will never be another for me. No one with the fire, the passion, the rage. No one with the beauty, kindness, and drive. There is only you. The only star in my sky. The light in my darkness.

RACHEL FALLON, *OF LIGHT AND FREEDOM*

I fell into a romantasy book and refused to climb back out

I would take her for a single night knowing that I'll lose her by morning, and I would hold on to her and never let go.

ALI HAZELWOOD, *BRIDE*

Throw a masquerade ball

Sadly, we can't be reading romantasy *all* the time – we must remember our real-world friends as well as our fae friends. But if you want to keep the romantasy vibe going, why not throw your very own romantasy-themed masquerade ball? Give everyone plenty of time to put together an outfit based on their favourite book, character or creature, complete with a dramatic mask, and decorate the party room with banner flags for your favourite kingdoms, draped fabrics, tall candles and stacks of romantasy books. Then enjoy an evening in the company of high lords, vampires, tyrant queens, charming rogues and cursed heroines.

Did you think you could stop me? I'll burn the world down to save her.

JENNIFER L. ARMENTROUT, *ORIGIN*

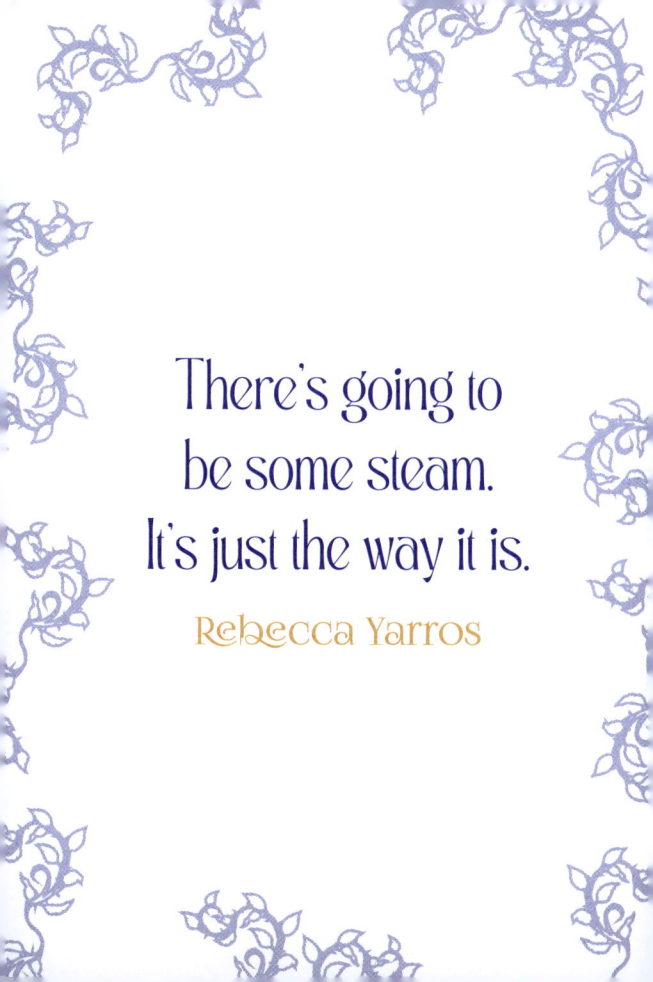

She could hardly deny that it felt real. And it was a darkness she was walking swiftly into. At least her eyes were open.

K. A. Linde,
The Wren in the Holly Library

I LOVE FLIRTING WITH DANGER AND CURSED MEN

She was my constant lantern when, like now, the world was dark and I didn't know which way to go.

PENN COLE,
SPARK OF THE EVERFLAME

When he bonded to his queen, he would settle for nothing less than someone who set his blood on fire.

NISHA J. TULI, *TRIAL OF THE SUN QUEEN*

ANOTHER DAY, ANOTHER MYTHICAL CREATURE TO TAME

My affections were dark,
possessive, all-consuming.

STACIA STARK,
A COURT THIS CRUEL & LOVELY

Curses, after all,
are made to be broken.

GEORGIA SUMMERS,
THE CITY OF STARDUST

Mood music

Create your own playlists for different moods or scenarios that will help you summon up the feeling of being in a romantasy world – even if you're just doing the housework. Perhaps there are songs that conjure up the feelings of lust and yearning that your star-crossed lovers have been tortured by. Or maybe there's an artist whose music puts you in mind of a dragon-training montage. Some songs give "long moonlit nights in the library", while others might summon up "entering the sorcerer's lair" vibes. Let the magic of music transport you to an enchanted realm.

YOU MAY WRITE ME POETRY, BUT MY DRAGON BURNS MY ENEMIES TO ASH

It doesn't take a blade to carve open a heart. It only takes a soft glance.

Chloe Gong,
Immortal Longings

I know we dance even after loss to cling to joy. I know we fight as a unit, side by side, because we are only as strong as our weakest. We cover each other, protect each other. We'd prefer to die fighting for what we believe in than live in the shadow of oppression.

J. ELLE, *ASHES OF GOLD*

I don't need therapy;
I need enemies-to-lovers
and an enchanted kingdom

Fire of my blood,
sun of my soul, I would raise
my armies in your defence
and I would stand by your
side though the Eversea
itself be against us.

THEA GUANZON,
THE HURRICANE WARS

She looked like dreams and nightmares and everything he'd ever wanted.

KATE DRAMIS, *THE CURSE OF SAINTS*

ALWAYS DREAMING OF DRAGONS

If you're the way my fate
finally catches up to me,
I can't fathom a more
beautiful end.

PENN COLE,
SPARK OF THE EVERFLAME

When you were supposed to seduce the enemy but accidentally fell for his dragon

Hints of cinnamon, leather and smoke

Every romantasy reading session comes complete with built-in atmosphere, but some well-chosen candles can heighten the drama and help immerse you in worlds of celestial courts and cloud academies, woodsmoke-scented cottages and moonlit glades. Look online for scents that match the mood you're after, or try making your own. Think sweet cinnamon, bitter orange, sage and pine, cedar and oak. You can even buy candles that smell like leather-bound books, so you can imagine you're in your very own high tower library.

We can do this dance until this world burns and the next takes its place, but I will still choose you.

AMBER V. NICOLE,
THE THRONE OF BROKEN GODS

The male's voice came out as a deep purr that made Lore think of an ice-cold river, one that would pull you under to its darkest depths if you dared dip a toe in.

Analeigh Sbrana,
Lore of the Wilds

He was death and rage
and fire and anyone stupid
enough to forget that would
be consumed by his inferno.

Kerri Maniscalco,
Kingdom of the Wicked

I LIKE MY BOOKS HOW I LIKE MY DRAGONS: SASSY, POWERFUL AND SCORCHING HOT

When I dwelled in the wanting, it felt like an ocean, endlessly vast and moving just beneath the surface of my skin. If I stayed there, I would be swept away.

MAIGA DOOCY,
SORCERY AND SMALL MAGICS

Never let anyone make you feel bad about the things you're capable of. Some will insist you step into the shadows to make them more comfortable. But I'll tell you a secret: there's enough light for us all.

RACHEL GRIFFIN, *THE NATURE OF WITCHES*

Magical training,
but make it shirtless and
emotionally charged

She wanted to rip down the sky
and shred it with her fingernails,
to pluck every star from the
fabric of heavens until fathomless
darkness matched the
void inside her.

EMILY THIEDE, *THIS VICIOUS GRACE*

You are the hurricane that has ravaged my heart, Rayna, and you are the only one who can put it back together.

MARIAH MONTOYA,
BY THE ORCHID AND THE OWL

Scale art

If you can't get enough dragons in your life, you can carry a tribute to your favourite mythical creatures along with you all day through the wonder of dragon-scale nail art. Iridescent varnishes can be embellished with black details to outline the scales and make them look 3D, or, if you don't trust that you have a steady enough hand, keep it simple and let the shimmering varnish remind you more subtly of your allegiance to your dragon. If nails aren't your thing, you could find iridescent papers to cover your journals, make bookmarks or even make simple jewellery with a hint of dragon-fire.

His eyes, when they meet hers, are like the storm. Perhaps he is not a boy at all, but some elemental thing, made by the crashing water and the endless thunder.

Kendare Blake,
Three Dark Crowns

Come out and play with me, my star. I know you're in there somewhere, burning away where you think no one can see you. Imagine how brightly you'd shine if you embraced all that fire.

Harper L. Woods,
What Lies Beyond the Veil

Part-time human, full-time daydreamer

Eldas kisses me like the creature of darkness that he is, determined to consume every last flicker of my light.

**ELISE KOVA,
*A DEAL WITH THE ELF KING***

What is more lovely, after all, than a monster undone with want?

S. T. GIBSON, *A DOWRY OF BLOOD*

I'm just a girl, standing in front of a romantasy book, asking it to destroy her emotionally

> If ruin was the price of having him,
> let him destroy me.

GENEVA LEE, *FILTHY RICH FAE*

She is not the end of anything, but the beginning of everything. He has been dead a long time, and she is his resurrection.

A. B. PORANEK,
WHERE THE DARK STANDS STILL

My hobbies include falling in love with fictional men and crying at fictional deaths

He was dangerous in all the right ways and I knew without doubt that the fire in his eyes would burn me up if I strayed too close.

Caroline Peckham, *The Awakening*

I've never been a religious man, but I will worship you in ways the gods will envy.

Olivia Rose Darling,
Fear the Flames

SHE'S READING FAIRY SMUT AGAIN

"If this is madness,"
she whispered
almost against his lips,
"drown me in it."

RUNYX, *GOTHIKANA*

"I have waited lifetimes for you," he said as if it was an oath he was swearing upon every star in the sky, every drop of water in the ocean, every soul in the entire universe. "I know it."

SCARLETT St. CLAIR,
A TOUCH OF DARKNESS

Heart full of longing,
bookshelf full of brooding,
morally grey men

He gazed up at her like
he was fire and she was fuel.

HANNAH WHITTEN,
THE FOXGLOVE KING

> She was as wild and delicate as a flower but as dangerous and ravishing as wolfsbane.
>
> — AMARIE H., *THE CURSED SOUL*

Create your own dragon hoard

If you feel your reading nook is missing that certain something to make it extra cozy, why not create your very own dragon "hoard"? Collect artwork, crystals, ornaments and incense that evoke the feeling of your favourite books, and create a display of them next to your reading area, preferably surrounded by fairy lights and candles. Think of it as an altar to the romantasy gods – your favourite authors – and make sure you come to pay tribute regularly.

YOU GAVE ME DIAMONDS; MY DRAGON GAVE ME WINGS

I was restless. There was a fire in my blood tonight and I couldn't seem to quell it.

Briar Boleyn,
On Wings of Blood

She reminded him of the sea: steal-your-breath beautiful on the surface, with the promise of untold depths beneath.

Kristen Ciccarelli,
Heartless Hunter

Romantasy is my love language

When I read a romance,
I can fall in love over
and over and over.

REBECCA YARROS

For those who feel small and quiet. Spread those wings and roar.

SARAH A. PARKER, *WHEN THE MOON HATCHED*

With him, I am forever a night-blooming flower, attracted and repelled by the heat of the sun.

HOLLY BLACK, *THE STOLEN HEIR*

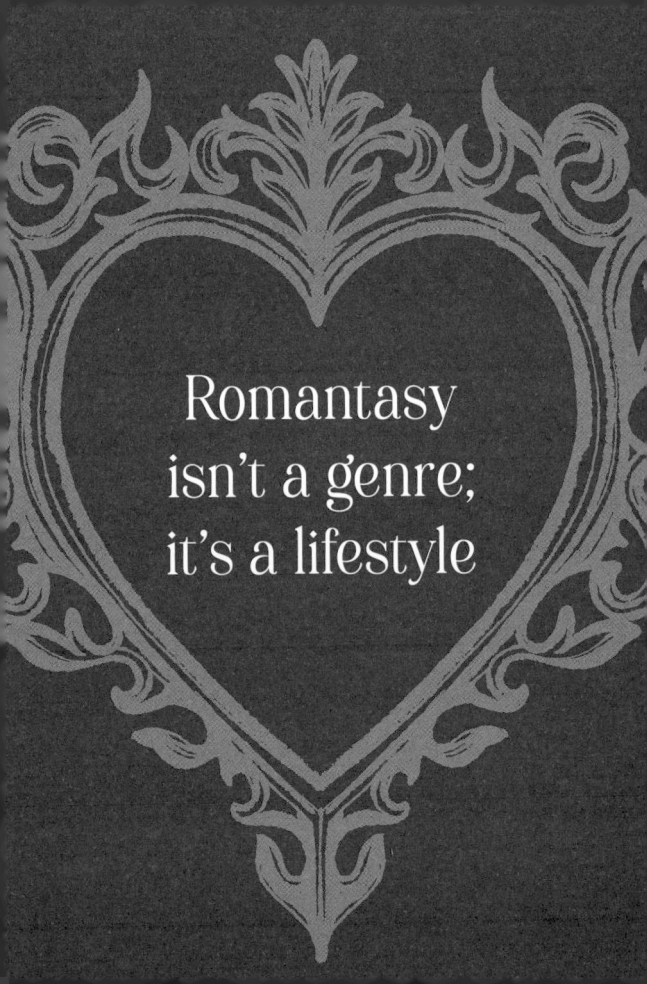

Bookish brews

Before settling down, brew yourself a warm drink, perhaps themed to the book you're reading. A spiced herbal tea might double up for elven tea; mulled wine could become bloodwine; a vanilla chai could be honeyed milk; or you could go for something "stronger" with your favourite spirit stepping in for firebrandy or dragon's breath. Let the ritual of it all help you sink further into the world of your book.

"Call us even. Call me crazy. I don't care. Just..." His eyes are pleading, brimming with emotion. "Just call me yours."

LAUREN ROBERTS, *RECKLESS*

Maybe no one was a hero.
Maybe I'd gotten it wrong from the
beginning. Maybe there were only
heroic moments and decisions and
we all had to keep choosing
those as best we could.

ANDREA STEWART,
THE BONE SHARD WAR

With a temper like mine, a girl is bound to get in trouble now and then... or often.

Nisha J. Tuli,
Trial of the Sun Queen

THE MORE DOOMED THE LOVERS, THE BETTER THE INEVITABLE ONE-BED SCENE

I couldn't be his savior;
I had enough to do
saving myself.

NAOMI NOVIK,
THE LAST GRADUATE

Love may give you strength, but retribution gives you purpose.

SAARA EL-ARIFI, *THE FINAL STRIFE*

It's giving "touch her and you die" vibes

It was as if something had
snapped inside him, some need that
he wasn't able to control, and
my kiss was the only cure.

HOLLY RENEE, *THE VEILED KINGDOM*

And then his arms were around me, and mine around him, and the two of us held each other for a minute and an eternity, like two halves reunited.

CARISSA BROADBENT, *THE ASHES AND THE STAR-CURSED KING*

Keep a romantasy quote grimoire

Find a suitably beautiful journal, and use it to write down the steamiest quotes and most tantalizing scenes from each book you read. You could categorize them into longing, enemies-to-lovers, friends-to-lovers, grumpy/sunshine and love triangles, or just collect together every line that makes you swoon. Take time to write them with calligraphic flourishes, sketches and pressed flowers, or scribble as quickly as you can if you're desperate to get back to the story. The important thing is that you have your own personal grimoire that you can return to whenever you want to bask in your favourite lines.

Girl dinner, but make it ancient scrolls, a blood oath and suppressed feelings

My name on his lips was like a prayer, if a prayer could be sensual. It was nearly enough to make me whimper.

Kate Golden,
A Dawn of Onyx

A true man won't cut you down as you fight your battles, nor will he fight them for you. A true man will help sharpen your sword, guard your back and fight at your side, in the face of whatever darkness comes.

HELEN SCHEUERER, *BLOOD & STEEL*

I read for the plot…
The plot is him shirtless
on a battlefield, having
just defended my honour

He was water, and
I was dying of thirst.

ALEXIS CALDER,
KINGDOM OF BLOOD AND SALT

As much as I loved him,
I loved myself more. And as I was
discovering, there was no end to
love – it was something which grew
and renewed endlessly, expanding to
encompass each new horizon.

SUE LYNN TAN,
DAUGHTER OF THE MOON GODDESS

Daydreaming in enemies-to-lovers again

Our love is stronger than time, greater than any distance. Our love spans across stars and worlds. I will find you again, I promise.

SARAH J. MAAS,
HOUSE OF SKY AND BREATH

Create your own fantasy

Why leave all the fun to the pros? If reading all about dragon-flight, danger and destiny has got you feeling inspired, maybe it's time to turn your hand to writing your own story. If you find the blank page intimidating, try just writing down some individual lines or phrases, and sketch out a few ideas first. Are there character names you love? Where is your story set – an icy, snow-bound sky kingdom, or a dark academy in a medieval city? Whether you want to spend time inventing an entire world, or you just want to get straight to the one-horse scene (no judgment here!), settle in for a cozy writing session and let your imagination run wild.

> We held each other close, life blazing in him and hellfire in me, immortal and monstrous – but in each other's arms, entirely human.
>
> MELISSA CARUSO,
> *THE IVORY TOMB*

I READ
FANTASY
BECAUSE
REALITY
HAS TOO
FEW
DRAGONS

You want to know something true? Something real? I'm in love with you. I have been since the night the snow fell in your hair and you kissed me for the first time.

REBECCA YARROS, *IRON FLAME*

I tried to prune a wild rose but only cut myself on her thorns. I tried to capture starlight but only engulfed myself in shadows. I tried so hard to keep you from dying that I forgot about living. I love all of you. And I cannot – I cannot live without you.

LYRA SELENE, *A CROWN SO SILVER*

My boyfriend brings me flowers; my dragon brings me skulls

"I am yours if you will have me, for as long as you want me."

Her lips parted softly, dark green eyes flitting between my own. "And if I want you until the end of time?"

"Then it will still not be enough."

GILLIAN ELIZA WEST, *RUIN*

Darkness was never as appealing as the light to most, but that didn't mean it was any less integral to life. Too much sunshine withered the soul. Balance was the key.

KERRI MANISCALCO,
THRONE OF THE FALLEN

No one understands me
like a fictional warrior
hero with a secret

There is nothing in this world I would not give up for you, no sacrifice I would not make.

Elizabeth Helen,
Bonded by Thorns

Revenge can't fill the hole in my heart; only she can.

Berlyn Hayes,
Prisoners of Betrayal

Romantasy book club

Sure, there are probably romantasy book clubs you could just join. But let's be honest – you're mainly here for the spice. If you're more interested in dissecting those devastating slow-burn moments and reliving your favourite steamy scenes than in talking about worldbuilding and literary merit, why not create your own book club? Arrange to meet fellow dark romantasy fans somewhere cozy where you can talk freely, and come prepared with a list of questions and scenes highlighted to prompt conversation. It might even introduce you to your new favourite fated lovers.

She wanted and wanted and wanted, so much and so deeply she feared her greed was boundless.

**ALLISON SAFT,
*A DARK AND DROWNING TIDE***

Dragons are a girl's best friend

The Romantasy Colouring Book: A Fantastical Journey of Colour and Creativity

Paperback
ISBN: 978-1-83799-604-9

The Romantasy Puzzle Book: 200 Brain-Teasing Activities Inspired by Magical Realms, Faraway Kingdoms and Enchanting Romances

Francis Nightingale
Hardback
ISBN: 978-1-83799-684-1

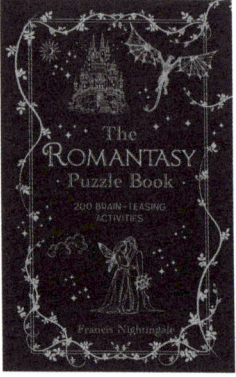

The Romantasy Cocktail Book: 52 Enchanting Recipes to Spice up Your Night

Francis Nightingale

Hardback

ISBN: 978-1-83799-730-5

In My Romantasy Era: Enchanting Quotes and Affirmations for Romantasy Fans

Hardback

ISBN: 978-1-83799-931-6

Have you enjoyed this book? If so, find us on Facebook at **Summersdale Publishers**, on Twitter/X at **@Summersdale** and on Instagram, TikTok and Bluesky at **@summersdalebooks** and get in touch. We'd love to hear from you!

www.summersdale.com

IMAGE CREDITS

Border (cover and throughout) © Media Guru/Shutterstock.com;
Brambles (cover and throughout) © GB_Art/Shutterstock.com;
Celtic pattern © Bourbon-88/Shutterstock.com;
Clouds © AlyonaZhitnaya/Shutterstock.com;
Dagger © DvViktoria/Shutterstock.com;
Dragon (cover and throughout) © Login_off/Shutterstock.com;
Heart frame © Oleksandra Klestova/Shutterstock.com;
Purple dragon, moon and stars © Shtefan Yelizaveta/
Shutterstock.com; Rose © LesiaArt/Shutterstock.com